Lies We Share

A Prologue

Ella Miles

LIES SERIES

Lies We Share: A Prologue

Vicious Lies
Desperate Lies
Fated Lies
Cruel Lies
Dangerous Lies
Endless Lies

1

LANGSTON

Five Years Old

"Langston!"

My name booms through the small house, rattling my tiny frame as I lie on the floor of the kitchen, staring up at empty cabinets. I wish these cabinets were filled with food, any food, to soothe my aching belly. I'd even take broccoli.

I don't know why my father has to yell so loudly. Our house is a tiny one-bedroom, one-bathroom, with a galley kitchen and a couch for a living room. My father could whisper in the house and I would still hear him.

I stop daydreaming about a stocked kitchen and pull myself up into a standing position. My bones pop and creak like an old man as I stand. It takes all of my willpower to walk into the living room where my father sits with a beer. He's staring up at the barely still working TV, watching some football game in between skipping channels.

I walk solemnly in front of him. There is only one reason

my father calls my name. It's better to do what he says or my fate will be worse. Giving in means the pain will end faster.

My three foot nothing body stops in front of my father. I don't speak, I know better than to do something that idiotic.

"I told you to take out the trash," my father says.

"I did, but—" *Why did I open my mouth?*

It doesn't matter that the trash doesn't fit in the trashcan, and the trash company won't take any extra bags outside the designated can.

"It reeks in here! You didn't take out the trash like I said."

Smack.

My body is already prepared for the impact as his hand thumps across my cheek. I hold back the tears, knowing I just have to hold on until I'm no longer in his sight before I cry. Crying gets me beaten worse.

"Take out the trash now! Before I beat your ass until you can't sit for a week."

I run into the kitchen and yank the lid off the trashcan that is almost as tall as me, before using both of my hands to pull the bag out. It gets stuck—probably a liquor bottle my father jammed into the can.

I sweat and grit my teeth to keep from making a sound, to keep the tears inside. If I let them out, I'll end up with a broken bone. I do everything I can to get the trash bag out myself.

Finally, the bag comes free, knocking me off balance. I fall back to the ground, the bag landing on my lap. It smells like canned tuna and sour beer.

I wrinkle my nose.

I can feel my father's stare. I scramble to my feet, heave the bag up with my two tiny fists and carry it out the front door. Once outside, I can take a breath. Father won't care how long I take; he just wants me out of his sight and the smell gone.

I let the bag fall to the ground, dragging it down the front stairs and down the driveway until I reach the full trashcan.

I consider my options: leave the bag next to the trashcan and get in trouble when the trash company doesn't pick it up, or find another way to get rid of it.

I look at the house across the street that also has its trashcan out on the end of their driveway. It doesn't look like it's overflowing.

Maybe mine will fit?

It's worth a shot.

I drag my bag across the pothole-riddled street, hoping the bag doesn't rip. The bags we use aren't the durable kind; they're the kind that tears if you jostle the bag the wrong way. There is a high probability I'll leak trash all over the street—then I'll really get my ass whooped.

By some miracle, I make it to the neighbor's trashcan without a significant rip. I lift the lid off their can—*there's room!*

I heave my trash bag up...

"What are you doing?" a girl says.

I drop the bag at the sudden voice, and it lands in the trashcan. I snap the lid shut.

I look over at the girl crouched behind a bush, which must be the reason I didn't see her when I walked over. She's covered in dirt. I can't tell if those are freckles on her cheeks or just more dirt under her hazel eyes and shoulder-length blonde hair. The only thing girly about her is her pink shirt with a picture of a pony wearing a tiara on it.

"Disposing of a body," I say, wondering how she's going to respond. I figure if she calls her parents or the police and tells them there's a body in the bag, the relief when they discover no body will bode better for me than the truth.

I also expect my words will get rid of her faster than the truth.

I don't expect her to cock her head, her eyes to light up, and a smile to lift her lips.

"What are you doing?" I throw her words back at her as I cross my frail arms in front of my body.

"Hunting."

I raise my eyebrows. "Hunting what? I don't see a gun."

Her eyelashes flutter at that, but she's not afraid. You can't be scared to grow up on a street like ours.

"I don't think a gun would help me."

"What are you hunting?"

"A spider—I think its home is out here somewhere, but it keeps coming into my room at night."

I'm intrigued by this girl who hunts spiders.

I look back at my house. I should go back.

And do what?

I don't have any toys.

I don't have any food.

This girl will be a good distraction.

"I'll help you," I say.

"I don't need your help."

"Have you found the spider yet?"

"No."

"Then you need my help."

"Fine, but you have to do what I say. I'm the one in charge."

I smile. "Deal."

I walk over to where she is now crouched down again, examining the outside of a window where there are cobwebs scattered across the corner of the window.

"So, what does this spider look like?"

"He's big and black and has a red spot on it."

"And where did you see this spider?"

"It crawled on the floor by my bed last night. He scared the

4

crap out of me. I'm going to find him. I think this is his web he uses to catch other bugs, and then he goes inside to sleep where it's warm." She points to a web along the windowsill.

"Uh-huh. What makes you think this web belongs to the same spider as the one you saw last night?"

That gets her thinking. "I don't know. Let's go inside and see if we can find a web there."

I nod and follow her into her house.

She starts crouching down in the living room.

"Where is your bedroom? Should we start there?"

She stops and looks at me with eyes that could kill. "This is my bedroom."

"Oh." She doesn't have a bedroom, either. She's just like me.

"Is that a problem? Can we not be friends because I don't have a bedroom? I'd like to see *your* bedroom then if you are too good for me."

I smile. I like how strong she is. She isn't embarrassed that she doesn't have a bedroom.

"Why are you smiling?"

"Because I sleep in the living room, too. I don't have my own bedroom either."

She smiles. "That's what I thought."

"Do you have any siblings?" I ask, sometimes kids have to share their couch with other kids.

"No, you?"

I shake my head.

That makes her smile more.

"Good, that means you need me to be your friend."

"I don't need you to be my anything. I don't need friends. I already have plenty of friends."

"Liar."

I frown. "I'm not lying!"

She takes my hand. "It's okay. I won't tell anyone that I'm your only friend."

I roll my eyes. *There is no winning with this girl.*

"Let's find this spider," I say.

She nods.

We both crouch down and search around the ten-foot by ten-foot square that is the living room.

"I found it!" she squeals.

I crawl over to where she's staring in the corner.

"You found the web and the spider, hunter."

She wrinkles her nose and sticks out her tongue. "Don't call me, hunter. My name is Liesel."

"Nope, your name is hunter."

"But that's a guy's name."

"Huntress?"

She nods, liking that better.

"What's your name?"

"Langston," I say my name out loud and shutter. My father calls me Langston. I only think of his beatings when I hear someone call me that name.

She notices; her eyes soft with sympathy as she looks at me more closely for the first time. She's probably noticing my swollen eye and bruise, but she doesn't say anything.

"Kill it before it gets away," I say, pointing to the spider that is now starting to crawl along the wall.

"I can't," her voice is quiet.

"Why not?"

"I just can't."

"You have to kill it. I think it's a black widow spider. It's poisonous. It could kill you if you don't kill it."

She thinks about my words for a second and lifts her pink sparkly flip flop to kill it, but then her foot slams back to her side. She can't kill the spider.

There is conflict in her hazel, gold speckled eyes. She needs the spider to be dead, but can't kill it herself.

I lift my worn, off-brand tennis shoes and slam it over the spider, killing it.

"Killer," she whispers.

"What?" I ask, terrified that she's going to be mad at me. I can't handle that. I really could use a friend.

"Your name. I'll call you killer. You'll call me huntress, and I'll call you killer."

I grin and nod, liking the nickname a lot better than her calling me Langston.

Just then, my stomach growls. I haven't eaten anything all day.

Hers growls louder a second later, making us both laugh.

"You got any food?" I ask.

She hesitates and bites her lip before she answers. "No."

She's lying—her first lie. I can tell. But when I look her over, I realize she needs whatever food she has a lot more than I do.

"It's okay. Enzo said he'd bike over later and bring me food."

"Enzo?"

"He's my friend."

"Sure, he is."

I laugh.

We both lay on the floor, leaning our heads against the foot of the couch.

Her smile drops as suddenly as it appeared. "How did you get that bruise on your eye?"

"That man I killed and put in your trashcan—he fought back. But don't worry, I won," I lie. Mine is an obvious lie, unlike hers. I'm five years old. I couldn't kill someone if I wanted to. The most I've ever killed is a spider. Although, I know my future. I suspect killing will become a means to survive.

She nods, pretending to accept my lie like I did hers, but she knows the truth. She knows my mother or father did this to me. It's the tale of too many kids in our neighborhood.

"I think we should make a pact," she says suddenly.

I sit up, looking at her. "Oh, yea? What kind of pact?"

"I'll hunt whatever needs hunting for you, and you'll kill for me." She holds out her pinky finger to me.

I'm not really sure why she thinks we need this deal. Maybe she needs me to kill her father for her like I need someone to do it for me. I'm not big enough to kill him now. But if she asks me to kill hers in a few years, I will gladly.

I link my pinky finger with hers. "And if either of us breaks our promise?"

"Then, the other gets whatever they want. They can take whatever they want of the other's. Demand anything. This is an unbreakable vow."

"Like in Harry Potter?"

"Yep."

"Fine, this is an unbreakable vow. I will always kill for you. And you will always hunt for me. Deal?"

We shake our pinkies together. "Deal."

2

LIESEL

Eight Years Old

The sound of the police siren sends chills down my spine as I try to sleep on the couch in the living room. I only have a light blanket, but I'm still drenched in sweat from the summer heat and lack of air conditioning. I don't know what time it is, but I'd guess past midnight. I should be asleep—I have school in the morning—but even without the sirens blaring, I wouldn't be able to sleep between the heat and my empty belly.

I wait for the sirens to disappear again, but they grow louder, closer.

I hold my breath as I hear the sirens just outside my house.

When you live where I do, sirens are never a good thing. Sirens aren't coming to save someone. They are coming to lock someone up or to drag the body off after an overdose or gunshot. The police never make it here in time to stop the suffering. Not in a poor area like this.

I start running out of oxygen, and still, the sirens don't leave. Their lights continue whirling, reflecting into the living room that serves as my bedroom.

I lift my head to glance out the window and gasp.

The police are entering Langston's home.

I jump up and run to the window and peer through the broken shades at the scene before me.

My mind races with all the horrible things that could have happened to the boy who has quickly become my best and only friend. I call him killer, but the truth is I don't think he's killed much more than a spider. I still call him that because it beats seeing the torment in his eyes when I call him Langston like his father does. Someday, Langston will earn the nickname I give him. I know that. But for now, it's still an innocent nickname—one that doesn't haunt him, or me, yet.

What happened?

Did Langston's father finally take things too far? Did he hurt him, injure him, kill him?

Please, no.

Please let it be his father. Please let him have drunk too much alcohol. Let him have alcohol poisoning or, better yet, be dead.

Let it be Langston's mother.

Just don't let it be my killer—Langston has to live.

I should wait inside my house, where I at least have the illusion of being safe.

I can't.

Not when I don't know if Langston is alive, hurt, or dead.

I run out the front door, not giving a damn about my own safety.

My feet are bare; my frayed T-shirt hangs down below my knees, hiding my shorts beneath, and my hair hangs in frizzy blonde waves. None of that matters—only Langston.

"Langston!" I shout, using his name instead of killer.

I run across the street, slipping between the two police cars that have arrived so far. I hear more approaching sirens in the distance.

I make it across the street. The front door is open. I should wait outside, but I can't.

I run up the uneven stairs full of cracks. I know each crack by heart, which makes it easy to avoid hurting my bare feet as I run.

Then I'm inside the small house already filled with too many people.

Three police officers.

Langston's father.

I don't see Langston.

"Langston!" I shout even though I shouldn't. I should blend into the shadows for as long as I can before being noticed. As soon as the police officers notice me, they'll escort me outside, and then I won't know anything.

The female officer turns at the sound of my small voice. Her lips thin in disappointment as she walks over to me. She squats down so she is eye level with me.

"I'm so sorry," she starts.

"No," I whisper. "He can't be dead."

I look past her, searching for the boy—the only one in my life who matters, who will ever matter.

She shakes her head.

What does that shake mean?

"Your mother—she didn't make it. She's in heaven," the officer says, putting her hands on my shoulders to comfort me.

I exhale a breath.

I should cry, show some emotion. This woman thinks I'm Mrs. Pearce's daughter, that I just lost my mother. She'll let me stay with Langston if I cry.

So that's what I do. I cry like I just lost a caring mother, instead of being relieved that my best friend is still alive.

The woman pulls me into a hug. That's when I spot him, and my heartbeat settles.

Langston is standing in shorts and no shirt, revealing his too-thin frame. His hair is a shabby mess on top of his head, and he's staring down at something.

His mother.

My heart breaks for him. He wasn't that close to her, but his mom was the only source of affection or love he got at home.

Now it will be just him and his father.

I keep the crying up, and Langston eventually looks at me. He laughs quietly when he sees my dramatic acting.

Finally, the woman releases me.

"I want to go see my brother."

"Of course, sweetie. You two should be together."

I walk over to Langston with tears still dripping out of my eyes.

"You're a terrible actress," he says teasingly when I walk over.

I wipe my tears on the back of my T-shirt. "I fooled her, so I can't be that bad."

He grins.

And then we link our hands. "Thank you," he says.

"For what?" I frown, not understanding why he's thanking me.

"For crying, even though you hate it, so you can be here with me."

I squeeze his hand. I'm beginning to think I'd do anything for this boy. Fake crying so I can hold his hand while he mourns his mother barely touches the surface of what I'd do.

3

LANGSTON

TODAY SHOULD BE the worst day of my life.

I'm burying my mother today.

Today is the worst day of my life, but not because today is my mother's funeral.

Today is the worst day of my life because of what I'm going to have to tell Liesel.

I'm wearing an oversized suit my father got at Goodwill and sitting in the front pew of the church next to my father.

There are a dozen or so people sitting behind us as the preacher talks. I don't listen. All I can think about is what I'm going to say to Liesel.

How am I going to break the news?

I can't even believe it myself.

I'm thankful for the time in the church. At first, I thought I wanted Liesel sitting next to me. Right now, I couldn't be happier that my father didn't allow it and that she's sitting three pews back. As long as we aren't together, I don't have to tell her.

Too soon, the funeral ends. The preacher stops talking, and my father and I stand as we follow the casket out of the church. The cemetery is next to the church, so we don't have to drive anywhere. We just walk to her grave with the small congregation of people behind us. I don't look back even though I can feel Liesel's stare, trying to reach out and comfort me.

I'm not the one who needs comfort, though.

Time moves too fast.

The preacher speaks more words.

My mother's casket is lowered into the ground.

And just like that—it's over.

My father gives me a stern look. "I expect you home in an hour."

I nod. He walks to the car and drives off.

A few people approach me, giving me their condolences.

I just stand, staring at my mother's gravestone like it's the most fascinating thing in the world. Reading my mother's name, dates of birth and death, and the words 'Beloved mother and wife' over and over to avoid what comes next.

Liesel doesn't speak. She just takes my hand like she did in the house three days ago when I woke to find my mother had overdosed on fentanyl.

I already know that isn't true. My father killed her. He slipped her the extra pills. He wanted her gone, so he got rid of her.

And then I feel something thorny being pushed in my other hand. I look down and see that Liesel has shoved a single rose-like flower into my hand.

"I'm sorry I couldn't afford more, but I think your mom would have liked it," she says.

I stare at the flower, similar to a rose but not. It's pretty— my mother would have liked it.

I look up at my mother's grave and then all the others around it. The surrounding graves have flowers. My mother's is bare.

The bastard didn't even spend money on flowers!

I feel the tear slipping down my cheek. I'll cry waterfalls later when I'm alone in the house. Right now, the single tear is enough.

I step forward, and Liesel steps right with me. Together we place the single flower at the base of my mother's grave.

"Goodbye, Mom," I whisper, keeping my tears and pain inside the best that I can.

Liesel pulls me into a hug. She isn't one for emotion. She's not a hugger, but in this moment, she is.

The embrace only makes me sob harder until there is snot running down my face and onto the shoulder of her black dress.

"I'm sorry." I let go of her as I suck the snot back in and try to compose myself. There are more important things to worry about than the loss of my mother right now.

Liesel's eyes flick right then left over my face. "What is it?"

How does she always know when something is wrong with me?

"We're moving," I spit out before I lose my nerve.

Her mouth falls, and tears spring into her eyes for the first time.

"But...your mom just died."

"Dad's remarrying some rich woman."

"Oh."

I don't have to tell Liesel what that means. I don't have to tell her that my father killed my mother. She can put the pieces together as easily as I did.

"He'll pay for this. Someday, he'll pay," Liesel says, her voice lower and grittier than before.

I nod, agreeing. One day my father will suffer for all of his sins—none worse than killing my mother.

Right now, I don't need to worry about my father though.

"Come on, we don't have much time." I grab Liesel's hand again and drag her over to the empty field behind the church.

"What are we doing?"

"I have a lot to teach you before I leave." Pain strikes my heart when I say the word—leave. I can't imagine leaving this girl. Not seeing her every day. Not talking. Not being in her life. It can't be true.

I let go of her hand and face her.

"Okay, first lesson, self-defense," I start.

"I know how to defend myself." She folds her arms and pouts, offended.

"Do you?"

She nods furiously.

We are relatively close in size. I have maybe an inch on her, but soon the boys at school will tower over her. They'll have more muscle and strength than she'll ever dream about. Not to mention all the creepy uncles and neighbors that Liesel will interact with in her life. She needs to be able to protect herself if I'm not here to do it.

I grab her, throwing my arms as tightly as I can around her, already knowing that I'm stronger than she is.

She wiggles in my arms. "Let me go, you asshole."

I hold her tighter.

"You can do this, huntress. Don't panic, think of a way to escape. Find my weakness and exploit it. Then run."

She stops struggling and thinks for a moment.

I search her eyes, trying to guess what she's going to do before she does it, preparing myself for her move.

Her knee pummels into my groin. I immediately release her, and she takes a step back, laughing lightly as I double over in pain.

"That's not funny," I say, my voice squeaking from the pain.

"It is to me."

"I told you to run after you got free."

"I know how to run. What's the next lesson you're worried about before you leave? Going to teach me how to kill too?"

We've never talked about it, but she knows what I'm capable of. I don't know how or why, but my future will involve killing people. It's not abnormal for our neighborhood; you either kill or be killed. My father tops the list of people that deserve to die. I'm too small to accomplish the task now, but soon...

I haven't killed yet, but I know how to hold a gun. I know how to use a knife; all I'm waiting for are my muscles to come in and the right opportunity.

But Liesel will never have to kill. I won't allow her soul to be in the torment to which mine is destined.

"No. We keep our promises. You'll hunt when I need you to."

"And you'll kill for me," she whispers back.

I nod. "I won't let you kill. I'll kill for you. No matter where I live. No matter where I go to school. I promise you."

She exhales a heavy breath.

"And you promise you'll never kill? You will call me and let me do it?"

"Yes," she says.

I'll hold her to that.

I don't have to worry about her killing to survive. I taught her the basics for protection, although, she'll need more lessons. What's more worrying is that she doesn't have any money or food. I've stolen food and money for us when we needed it. None of our parents can provide such simple things. At eight, we already have to feed ourselves.

I glance at my watch. Forty-five minutes until Dad said I needed to be home—it's not enough time.

"You need money," I say. I'm hoping that after my dad

remarries his new wife will be gracious enough to give me money to help support Liesel. But until then, I need to ensure Liesel has money for food.

She opens her mouth to disagree but then snaps it shut. She knows she needs money.

"What do you suggest?"

"We are going to steal it from someone who doesn't need it. Okay, huntress?"

"And where are we going to find someone around here who doesn't need money?"

I frown. I honestly have no idea.

"You're the huntress. Do you have any ideas?" I ask, embarrassed that I don't have an idea of how to help her.

She smiles. "Maybe."

I grin along with her.

"Do you have money for bus fare?" she asks.

I reach into my pocket and pull the twenty-dollar bill out —the only money I have left.

"This enough?"

"It'll have to be."

We spend the next twenty minutes on the bus driving toward the beach. We've ridden the bus this way before, but usually to enjoy the beach, not to steal.

We stand on the crowded beach. I suggested we go to an area with shops and stores, but Liesel disagreed.

"Okay, we're here. Nothing but tourists for miles."

She grins. "Exactly. Tourists swimming in the ocean, leaving their belongings on the beach. And tourists always have cash."

I suck in a breath. "I hope you're right."

"I am. I hunted, it's your turn to go in for the kill."

I laugh. "Stay right here. I'll be back soon with plenty of moola."

She stands on the edge of the beach as I jog along the tourists' belongings, looking for an easy target.

Liesel was right—there are unattended bags everywhere. But if I start going through belongings, I'm going to draw attention to myself. So rather than going through every bag, I pick my targets carefully, only selecting bags where the wallets are already in plain sight.

I snatch a wallet and pull out the cash before dropping it back down before anyone notices.

I do this three more times, collecting almost two hundred dollars and then run back to Liesel. It should be enough for a while, but not enough to grow up on. She needs money for years. Money to feed her, clothe her, send her to dance classes or let her join the softball league. Money she'll never have. Money I'll never be able to give her.

"Here," I say, shoving the money into her hands.

"Wow, that's a lot of money. Um…maybe you should keep some of it."

"I won't need it where I'm going."

She nods slowly in understanding and fists the money.

I glance at my watch. I'm officially a half-hour late. I know the beating I'll have to endure for being late, but I don't care. Tomorrow, we leave. Tonight, I'm spending every second with this girl.

4

LIESEL

We sit in comfortable silence on the bus ride home as I hold more money in my fist than I've ever held in my life because of this boy—this boy I'm about to lose.

It's more than him just moving away; there is something else happening. I don't understand what it is, but I can feel it in my bones. After tonight, everything changes.

The bus stops. We climb off and start walking the five blocks to our houses.

"You need to go home?" I ask.

Langston looks down, shuffling his feet with his hands in the pockets of his suit.

"No. I think we should camp under the stars tonight. One last epic night together."

"We don't have any camping equipment. How are we going to camp?" I really wish he'd stop insinuating that this is the end. We'll see each other again; it will just be different and less frequent.

"It's summer. I'll get us a thick comforter to lay on and some snacks. We can camp in the woods behind your house."

"Okay."

We separate at our houses.

I walk in the front door already knowing my mother has to work and isn't home. I glance out back as I enter and see Langston sneaking in the backyard a few minutes later.

He lied.

His father expects him home. I can feel it in my bones. But I'm too selfish to give up my last night with Langston so that his father doesn't beat him.

I quickly change into jean shorts and the T-shirt Langston gave me for my birthday that has a warrior princess on the front. The princess looks like she's about to go hunting. I pull my hair up in a ponytail and consider where I should hide the money we just stole.

I decide on the floorboard beneath my bed and shove the money deep inside, hoping my mother doesn't find it.

I walk back outside and find Langston already waiting. He too changed into more casual clothes—ripped jeans, a black T-shirt, and baseball cap. Years of sneaking around have made it easy for him to quickly step in and out of his house without his father noticing.

"Ready, killer?"

He smiles as I say his nickname. He swings a backpack over his shoulder, and then we head into the woods behind my house.

The sun is just beginning to set as Langston lays out the large blanket from his backpack.

We sit down on the blanket, surrounded by trees. For a moment, it feels like we are in our own little world. The real world no longer exists.

Langston pulls two Snickers bars out of his backpack and tosses one to me. I catch it with a smile.

Snickers are our favorite. They're cheap and filling and delicious.

"So, where are you moving to exactly?" I ask, biting into my candy bar.

Langston's eyes cut to me with a wary expression. "Palm Beach."

"Oh, wow. So this woman is really rich."

He nods and stops eating.

I do the same.

"I don't want you to worry, Liesel. This isn't the end. Our relationship won't change. We just won't see each other as often, but we can still count on each other. Always."

"I know."

"Maybe we shouldn't talk about this anymore tonight. Tomorrow is for goodbyes and tears; tonight is for making memories."

"Yea, we should enjoy our last night before you move."

"What should we talk about?" I take another bite of my Snickers bar, savoring each bite.

He lays back on the blanket.

I do as well.

We stare up at the sky, now shades of orange and red—the last moments before the sun sets.

"About a future that we can control. One where we aren't poor. One where we can live the life we want."

I frown as I look over at him. "But we never dream. What's the point?"

"The point is that the one benefit of my new life is that I just might be able to get us the life we want someday."

I take the last bite of my Snickers bar. He does the same.

Langston is so optimistic. His life might change for the better, but I'm destined to be stuck in this town forever.

I just smile at Langston. I don't care what we talk about tonight. I only want to spend it with him.

"You start. What do you want, killer?"

"First, I want everyone to call me killer. I want to be the

23

strongest badass I know. I want to be in complete control and be able to take on any foe."

As he speaks, I know that will someday come true.

"What about you?" he asks.

I stretch my arms up and place them behind my head, thinking about a question I've never thought before. Most eight-year-olds have already thought about what they want to be when they grow up. They dream of becoming doctors, teachers, president, astronauts. I just dream of a day when I won't have to worry if the meal I just ate is going to have to last me days or hours.

"I just want to live in a world where I have enough money to buy as much food as I want and have a real bed in my own bedroom."

"That's not a dream. That's going to happen. Dream bigger. What job do you want?"

"Lawyer," I answer automatically. That seems like the kind of job where you can make a change in other people's lives.

"Where do you want to live? Beach, mountains, city?"

"Definitely the beach." I like Miami's warm weather. I can't imagine living anywhere else.

"Me too. The mountains are too cold, and the city is too busy. I want to live on my own private island."

My eyebrows raise. "We're really dreaming big."

"Absolutely. But I can't figure out what I want my house to look like."

"Ooh, I can help with that. It should be big and made of glass," I say as I relax my arms to my side again.

"Glass? Doesn't that mean it will be easier to break?"

I laugh. "No, it will be full of light. You'll have views of the ocean from every room."

"I like that. And it needs a big kitchen. One that can cook a meal for a dozen people."

"And an infinity pool!"

"And a huge balcony!"

"A bathroom outside!"

"A deck covered in vines and greenery that makes it feel like we are living in the jungle."

I look up at the stars.

"And the clearest view of the moon and stars," I say.

Langston's hand intertwines with mine. "That's the most important part."

"So that's your house. Where will I live?" I ask.

"In the house with me."

"You mean as your wife?"

He shrugs. "Maybe, or maybe we'd live there as friends. Would it be so bad, being married to me?"

"I don't know. We're eight. And all the marriages I've seen have failed. I don't want us to fail."

"Maybe we should kiss and see how we like it. That way, we'll know if we should be married or just live there as friends."

I've never thought of kissing a boy before. But I know Danica in my class kissed Ian last week.

"Okay, kiss me then." I sit up, leaning on one elbow.

Langston leans on his elbow, facing me. It's beginning to get dark outside, but I can tell he's nervous. He's hesitant. I don't understand why. It's only a kiss.

"Kiss me, killer."

Then his lips are pressed against mine. Our noses bump. Somehow, I end up biting his bottom lip.

"Ow," he says as we both pull away.

Then we laugh.

"Well, I guess that answers that," I say.

"Yep, friends it is," Langston says.

I smile, as we both lay back on the blanket and start trying to make images out of the stars.

For some reason, I can't get that kiss out of my head. Langston was my first kiss. It seemed terrible. I don't understand why anyone would want to kiss. But then again, I'm eight.

I snuggle up to Langston as we begin to drift off to sleep. I feel his steady heartbeat. I know what he's risking staying with me tonight. I won't let him get hurt for me. It may not be part of our pact, but I make a silent promise to myself to never let him get hurt. Tomorrow, I'll do what I can to keep that vow.

―――――

I wake up before dawn, knowing that Langston will wake as soon as the sun touches his face. I have very little time to do this.

Carefully, I rise off Langston's arm.

He doesn't move.

I smile at my sleeping boy. Then I grab the T-shirt, hat, and jeans he took off when it got too hot last night. He's sleeping on the blanket only in his boxers.

I run off back to my house through the early morning hours. Once inside, I quickly throw on Langston's clothes.

His jeans and T-shirt fit pretty well since we are about the same size. Then I pull my hair up in a bun and shove it under my hat.

I look at myself in the mirror in the bathroom. Everything girly about me is gone. If I have to speak, this won't work. But I have to try. I have to try to protect the boy who always protects me.

I run across the street as the sun begins to climb.

I glance back and don't see Langston following me. He's going to be pissed, but I don't care. I have to do this for him, just like he would for me.

I take a deep breath when I reach the front door, trying to prepare myself. I've dealt with more pain than most eight-year-olds have. I know what it feels like to be hungry. To sleep alone. To fear someone will break in and hurt you at night.

But I've never been physically hurt before.

I push the hat down as low as I can over my eyes and push the door open loudly. I practically stomp inside, ensuring that anyone inside can hear me.

"I told you to be home an hour after the funeral," Langston's father says in a booming voice.

I don't look up, but I see his boot covered feet in front of me.

"I had to stay up all night to get your shit packed because you ran off."

He wasn't worried where Langston was. Missing free labor and not being able to sit back and drink beer all night were his only concerns.

"Look at me, boy!"

I don't.

That pushes him over the edge.

Slap.

I feel it hard across my cheek. My instinct is to run. Or, at the very least, try and fight back to protect myself.

I can't. I have to endure this for Langston. Spending his final night with me shouldn't get him beaten.

"You stupid fucking son of a bitch."

A punch to my chest knocks me to the ground. I land hard on my ass. I'm going to have a bruise in both places.

I focus my energy on keeping my face pointed at the ground to hide my true identity from Mr. Pearce. From the smell of alcohol oozing off his breath, I doubt he'd look close enough to notice, though.

Kick.

My body flings from his boot in my back. I'm not much of a crier, but that does it. I can't hold back my tears. For the first time, I realize why Langston is a crier. There is no other way to deal with this kind of pain except to cry.

I dissolve into my body as the pain wrecks me. My sensitive skin bruises while my ribs crunch as he kicks me over and over.

I've lost track of how many times he's kicked me.

His curse words have all muffled together.

Without warning, he grabs my arm and forces me into a standing position.

"Get out of my sight. I can't look at you. Clean yourself up and come back when you are presentable." He releases my arm, and I stumble, trying to remain on my feet.

The world is spinning; tears stream down my cheeks, everything in my body hurts. But somehow I stay upright.

"Cynthia will be here at five to pick us up and take us to our new home. If you are one minute late, I'll beat you until you're dead. Understand, Langston?"

I nod. Even if I wanted to speak, I couldn't.

"Get out!" he yells.

Finally, I run.

Every step I take requires all of my energy, to put one foot in front of the other, to keep from falling flat on my face.

This is Langston's life. This will always be his life until he's old enough to put a stop to it. He might be getting a fancier house to live in, but it won't stop his father.

At least I was able to prevent one more beating he had to endure. If I could, I'd take all the pain for him, but I can't.

As soon as I'm out of the house, I consider my options.

I thought I'd be able to go back to my house afterward. I could change clothes, put on a couple of bandaids and tell Langston I fell off my bike or something. But there is no hiding what I did—no hiding the bruises, the blood, the tears.

Langston will be pissed at me. He'll be angry and might even confront his dad, which would make everything I did moot. I'm not going to let that happen.

Yesterday was about making memories together.

Today was supposed to be about saying goodbye. About finding a way to connect in our new normal.

New tears spring.

We just lost our last day together because of me.

But I saved him from a beating. It was worth it. Even if I don't say goodbye.

I can't stay here.

Langston will eventually go home after he looks for me. I just have to make sure he shows up by five o'clock.

I run into my house and find a utility bill on the counter. I turn the envelope over and grab a marker before writing Langston a note.

Killer,

I had to go with my mom to work today. I'll try to make it back before you leave at five. If I don't make it back in time, I'll see you soon.

—Huntress

I grab some of the cash Langston and I stole, and then I leave. I'm not sure if I'll return in time to see Langston before he leaves, but I can't spend the entire day with him. He'd figure it out, and that would break me worse than Mr. Pearce's boot did.

The seconds, minutes, hours drag as I ride the bus to the mall and buy some new clothes that fit me, covering my arms and legs. I look at myself in the mirror in the public bathroom. The only visible mark now is where he grabbed my neck.

I brush my hair so it hangs down over my neck, making it that much harder for anyone to notice.

Finally, I take the four-thirty bus back home.

I don't know if I'll make it in time to see Langston before he leaves. I leave it up to fate.

I walk down our street at ten til five.

I'm not sure what to do. *Do I go over to Langston's? Or do I just go to my own house and try to forget about the boy?*

"I didn't think you'd show," Langston says from his house's doorstep, making my decision for me.

"I'm sorry, I did everything I could to get back. Mom needed me to help her clean houses—"

"Liar."

I frown.

"Your mother got home at noon. Want to try another lie, or do you want to tell me why you didn't spend my last day here with me?" He stands up and starts to approach me.

A vein is popping in his forehead, but he's wearing a T-shirt and shorts, and I don't spot any visible bruises.

I exhale a sigh of relief. I saved him from a beating. I would give up my last day with him over and over again if it meant I could spare him pain.

"I'm waiting. What lie are you going to tell me, Liesel?"

Liesel? He's pissed. He never calls me Liesel.

"Hugh, down the street, invited me over. I couldn't say no. He's going to be my only friend once you're gone."

"You're going to replace me, just like that? Like I mean nothing to you?"

I don't answer. How he can think that I lied about being with my mother but not about being with a friend is unbelievable. Why wouldn't I want to be here for my last hours with him?

He shakes his head. "I can't believe we were ever friends."

His words hurt worse than my cracked ribs.

I feel the burning of a tear in my eyes, but I don't let it out.

I swipe my hair to one side, revealing the bruise, revealing the truth.

But Langston won't even look at me. He's so irate.

"Langston! Time to go," Mr. Pearce says as a new Mercedes sedan pulls up.

Mr. Pearce walks to the front passenger side. A beautiful woman sits in the driver's seat—his new wife.

Langston still doesn't look at me. He just starts walking to the car.

"Langston," I whisper, hoping he'll look at me.

He'll give me a hug.

He'll say we are still best friends.

That he'll call.

Take care of me.

That this changes nothing.

Instead, he climbs into the back of the car without a word, without a glance back.

I watch in horror as the woman drives off with my best friend. I'm left stunned.

He left without a goodbye.

I hate him.

I shouldn't have taken the beating for him. It wasn't worth it.

I. Hate. Him.

I fall to the ground in a crumpled ball.

I hate him.

But that's a lie too. I can't hate him. Not yet. Soon though, I promise to hate him, to make it true. Because everything between us was a lie.

5

LANGSTON

Fifteen Years Old

I've spent the last few years pretending that I didn't know who Liesel Dunn was. That when her mother took a job as a maid in my friend Enzo's house recently and they moved into his guest house, that I didn't know her. I pretend that at one point she wasn't the most important person in my life.

I pretend she was just a girl, just like all the rest.

A girl I would try to kiss, maybe even one day fuck before moving on to the next girl, and then the next and the next.

I pretend that Liesel means nothing to me. I pretend I don't ask Enzo about his new roommate because I care but just because I have a fascination with all girls. I'm a horny bastard, after all. That's all it is.

Zeke truly hates her. He thinks she's a snob. He doesn't know that she's broken. That she only has money because I give money to Enzo, who gives money to her.

Enzo, on the other hand, likes Liesel. *But what do I care?*

He can have the lying whore if he wants.

I don't hate her—I just don't care anymore.

Liesel has spent the last several years either ignoring me or hating me. She also pretends I was never a part of her life. Yet, she still hangs out with the three of us constantly.

So annoying.

"I'm going to need you tonight," Enzo says as he slams his locker shut.

I pull my algebra textbook out of my locker. "Just tell me the time and place."

Enzo nods.

I've been working for Enzo for the last year. I always knew I would. It was my destiny, as it was Zeke's. The three of us will conquer the world together. Threatening, stealing, killing to keep the empire that Enzo will one day inherit from his father.

We are the bad guys now.

"Do you need me?" Zeke asks.

Enzo turns to him.

"I could really use an outlet." Zeke pounds his fist into his other hand.

"Who are you guys taking down?" Liesel asks, wrapping her arms around Enzo's neck.

He kisses the back of her hand.

"Nothing you need to worry about, Liesel," Enzo says.

Liesel sighs and lets go of him as she makes her way to the middle of the group. She folds her arms as she looks into each of our eyes, trying to get answers. I don't think she wants to know because she wants to judge us. It's more because she's a nosy bitch who wants to be able to control my life like she did when we were little.

"Finally going to get this one his first kill?" Liesel asks, gesturing in my direction.

I seethe. She doesn't know that I've already earned her

nickname for me. I've killed. I don't know if tonight's mission is to kill, but if Enzo requires it of me, I will.

My soul is already lost. I'm evil, and I like it. I won't let Liesel or anyone else change me.

Zeke laughs. "Langston isn't capable of killing a fly, sweetheart. If anyone does the killing, it will be me."

Liesel's eyes dart from Zeke to me. Zeke's words are true. He's killed the most of all of us so far. He's the biggest, the oldest, but Enzo and I will catch up soon. The only reason I don't have as big of a number as Zeke is because I do most of the behind the scenes work. I'm the most skilled with a computer. I've become both the hunter and the killer.

Liesel searches for the truth in my eyes, but she can no longer read me as easily as she once could.

When she doesn't find what she's looking for, she gives up and turns to Enzo.

"Walk me to class," Liesel says, shoving her textbook into Enzo's hands with a wink.

She tosses her blonde curled hair over her shoulder as she loops her hand into the crook of Enzo's arm, and he starts leading her away. I'm left to stare at her ass in a tight black dress with wedge heels, remembering her full face of makeup.

What the hell was that?

The only time I've ever seen her wear a dress was for my mother's funeral. I've never seen her wear a dress, or makeup, or style her hair like this. High school has changed her. Money has changed her.

Zeke makes a whipped sound at Enzo, who just flips him off as they round the corner.

My blood boils.

I'm not jealous, just pissed. I didn't think she'd become this fake just to get into Enzo's pants.

Not that he cares about her in that way. He might fuck

her a couple of times, but he doesn't love her. He'll fuck her and then expect her to go right back to being friends like they are now.

Three hours later, I spot Liesel waiting for Enzo to walk her to lunch.

I can't take it anymore.

"If you're just looking for someone to break that sweet hymen of yours, look no further," I say as I approach her with a laugh.

Liesel folds her arms and stares at me like I'm a demon she wishes she could send to hell.

"Why would I want to fuck a puppet like you when I can have sex with the king?"

I laugh harder. "Enzo? Really? You think he wants to fuck you?"

"Yes. He does."

I shake my head as I put one hand on the wall behind her, leaning close but not too close.

"Enzo's like me. He's a fuck 'em and leave 'em type. I don't think your pretty little heart can take it."

I tug on her blonde curls—I can't resist.

She bats my hand away.

"I'm tougher than I look. And I know how to wrap a guy around my finger. If I want Enzo, I'll have Enzo."

I laugh. "Enzo Black will never be yours."

She pushes off the wall. "Don't worry, I'm not planning on stealing him away from you guys. You and Zeke wouldn't survive without your fearless leader telling you what to do all the time."

I growl.

She smirks victoriously.

"I'm calling in our pact," I say, preventing her from walking away.

"Our pact? Oh, you mean the pact we made when we were five? Before I knew you were a giant asshole?"

"Friday night. Meet me at Enzo's. We're going hunting."

She shakes her head and stomps off.

It's a test to see if she'll come—if deep down she still cares.

Now I just have to wait to see if she shows up or not.

6

LIESEL

I FINISH the braid down the back of my head and then stare at myself in the mirror. I look like Katniss with my braid, all black clothes, and hunter mentality. All I need now is a bow and arrow and I'd be a true hunter.

Still, I feel ready. This day came a lot sooner than I expected it to. I expected I'd be older, about to leave this town for good. On the other hand, this day couldn't come fast enough.

I know without Langston telling me what today is about. There is only one reason he would call on our pact after years of ignoring and hating each other.

To kill his father.

I hate Langston.

I hate that he ignores me.

I hate that he is an obnoxious flirt in school.

I hate that he kills and has become Enzo's little henchman.

But most of all, I hate that he still knows me better than anyone. A part of me still wants to care, still yearns to return to the friendship we once shared.

I hate myself most of all for still caring.

That's not what killing Langston's father is about, though. I'm not doing this for Langston. I'm doing this for me. For the little girl who got beaten by this horrid man.

I will ensure that he dies, just like the part of me that died that day.

I step out of the small guest house on Enzo's property. I'm not sure if Langston invited Enzo and Zeke to take part in the hunting and killing of his father or not. Enzo and Zeke understand. They would want to help us kill him. They would be able to do the job as well as me, but that isn't what this is about.

Enzo and Zeke didn't experience the abuse. They didn't spend years with the monster. They have their own demons, but not like Langston and I do. For Langston and me, this is personal in an entirely different way.

I wait outside as the sun begins to set to see who is going to show up.

Langston appears from the side of Enzo's house. He must have come around back instead of through the house.

"Where are Enzo and Zeke?" I ask.

He shakes his head. "They aren't coming. This is just about the two of us."

I nod.

His hardened, cool eyes examine me from head to toe. I've never seen Langston so calm and cool. Usually, he has an air about him, a lightness. Not today.

"What happened to your dress?"

"I didn't think it was appropriate for hunting."

He chuckles. "We aren't literally going hunting. That's not how you catch a monster."

"How do you catch a monster, then?"

He shrugs. "You're the hunter. You come up with a plan. I'll just kill him once you lure him away."

What he's not saying is that he's too close to the man he plans on killing. If he comes up with the plan, he'll make a mistake because he's not thinking clearly. He needs me to help him.

"Where is he tonight?" I ask.

"There is some party that he and the stepmonster are having. We won't be able to kill him until after, maybe not even tonight. Tonight might just be about strategizing how to kill him. It—"

"No. He dies tonight."

Langston stares at me, really looking at me for the first time in years.

We may hate each other, but we know the depths of each other's pain. Killing Langston's father might be one of the few areas we still agree on.

"Tell me what your plan is," Langston says, his voice firm and yet hauntingly begging me to tell him how to end his pain and suffering.

My wheels start turning.

I know what we have to do, even though I sort of hate it.

"Go borrow Enzo's most expensive suit," I say.

Langston frowns. "I'm not wearing a suit. I'm not going to that asshole's party. I'm not—"

"Do you want to kill your father tonight or not?"

He sighs and runs his hand through his hair. "Yes, but—"

"This is the only way he dies tonight. We go to the party; we pretend that we are the perfect couple doing exactly what your stepmonster wants, and then we kill him."

"There will be too many witnesses."

"No, there will be too many suspects."

Langston peers into my eyes. Neither of us blinks. His pain oozes off him, letting me know how desperately he needs this tonight. He can't wait. We can't fail.

"We won't fail," I say.

His lips thin into tight lines. He gives me a solemn nod and then heads back to Enzo's house.

I turn and head inside, already pulling the braid down. At least my hair will now turn into soft waves, so the braid wasn't a complete waste.

I dig through my closet until I find the perfect dress for tonight. A dress that Enzo bought me, just like every other piece of clothing in this closet. I'm so lucky my mother found this job and that Enzo helps me when he can.

I quickly change, apply makeup, fluff my hair and then run out the door just as Langston starts out the house.

He doesn't see me at first, so I get to watch him without feeling embarrassed that there is a little line of drool on the corner of my mouth.

The suit doesn't fit him perfectly. It's slightly too big in the shoulders and just a hair too short in the legs. But no one will notice because the boy wearing the suit demands to be seen. His tousled blonde hair, bright blue eyes, and toe-curling grin capture my gaze. Even with the look of complete determination on his face, he shines brighter than the sun.

I don't understand how he can pull off that look. And I have a feeling as he grows older, more and more women are going to fall for his charms. More and more women are going to want him.

Good thing I don't want him. I could turn into a jealous bitch if I have to watch years of girls parade themselves in front of Langston.

Langston finally looks up. He stops walking. The brightness is gone when he looks at me. That's who I am—I steal the life out of people.

He continues walking to me. He doesn't comment on my appearance, and I don't comment on his.

"Does your plan involve a way to get to my stepmonster's house? Because the bus doesn't stop anywhere near there."

Langston hardly ever stays at his house. Instead, he's almost always here at Enzo's.

"I thought we'd drive," I say with a smile.

"We aren't sixteen. Neither of us has a driver's license or has ever driven on our own before."

I roll my eyes. "You know how to use a gun. You know how to hack into any computer. You've most likely killed before. I don't think driving without a license even registers on the list of bad things you've done."

He frowns.

"Are you scared? Think you can't drive without wrecking us? I could always—"

"No, I'm driving. We'll take the Porsche."

I smile—my favorite of all Mr. Black's cars.

We head inside Enzo's house. Luckily, Enzo and his father are at the club working, so we don't have to ask permission to use the car. We just take it.

Enzo wouldn't care.

And if Mr. Black knew that we were killing Langston's father tonight, he'd probably approve. The only bigger monster than Langston's father is Enzo's father.

We both climb into the Porsche. Langston doesn't hesitate. He puts the car in reverse and backs out of the garage.

I flip on a pop song.

Langston growls and switches it to rap.

"Passenger gets to pick the music," I say, flipping it back.

"You're ridiculous."

He steps on the gas too hard, and we lurch forward.

"Easy, tiger. We don't want to get us killed before we even arrive."

He lightly taps the gas, and then we are driving like the grown-ups we were forced into being far too young.

Annoyed with my music choice, he turns off the radio. Then his eyes grace the hem of my mid-thigh angelic dress.

It's covered in pretty white lace—the only part of it that hints that I'm still part girl. The rest of me is all woman. I developed early, already with plenty of curves at my hip and enough cleavage to draw in the most saintly of men.

"Why did you start wearing dresses, Liesel?"

There he goes calling me Liesel again.

I stare out the window. I started wearing dresses and acting girly when Enzo offered to pay for a new wardrobe for me, when I started a new school filled with rich snobs. The truth is I started wearing a dress because I liked the attention it gives me. I'm tired of blending in. Dresses make me feel like I'm more powerful than I really am.

"To drive you wild."

He grunts.

"Is it working?"

"What do you think?" he snaps.

Yes.

No.

I honestly can't read him well any more.

The conversation ends, though, as we pull up into the ridiculous circular drive in front of Langston's stepmom's house. Each of our doors is opened by a valet, and I take an offered hand helping me out of the car like we are about to attend a grand ball instead of a house party in Miami's richest area.

As soon as I get out of the car, I feel Langston brushing the valet's hand away from mine. He takes my arm carefully, like he's afraid that touching me is going to cause his hand to fall off.

I grab his arm more forcibly. "Holding my hand isn't going to kill you."

"Pretending that you're my girlfriend might."

I narrow my eyes. "If you don't want my help, then you can do this yourself."

"Fine, I'm sorry. Let's just get this over with."

I smile. "Follow my lead."

I spot our target and walk over to the stepmonster, who is talking excitedly with a group of chatty women. This will do perfectly to make our introduction.

"Introduce me to your stepmom with your charming smile," I say.

He frowns.

"Just trust me. Introduce me, I'll do the rest."

Langston leads me over and clears his throat as he approaches. "Ladies," he smiles at the women, laying on the charm. Then he looks to his stepmom. This part will be the hardest. "Mother, I'd like to introduce you to my girlfriend, Liesel Dunn."

He calls his stepmom 'mother' like she likes as he puts his hand on the small of my back with a bright, charming smile.

"It's a pleasure to meet you, Mrs. Pearce. I've heard so much about you."

Mrs. Pearce looks at me, hesitantly. She likes that Langston is here, that he called her mother, and that I look like a high-class girlfriend in my expensive dress. I just need to sell that I have money just like her, and then she'll approve of her stepson's choice in women.

"I'm sorry we were late. Langston had to pick me up on Fisher Island," I say, giving Enzo's house address. She doesn't have to know that the only reason my address is the same is because I live in the guest house while my mother works in the main house as a maid.

"Oh, it's a pleasure to meet you, my dear." Her eyes light up as she looks from Langston to me.

I gently lean into Langston's side, selling the appearance that we are boyfriend and girlfriend.

We pretend to be interested in what the women are saying for a while, before excusing ourselves.

"How did that help anything?" Langston asks.

I grab his tie and pull him into the nearest bedroom before I kick the door shut behind me.

"Your stepmom is happy. She'll think I'm good for you and start to trust you a little more. She'll tell your dad, who won't believe her and will come to us."

I sit on the edge of the bed. "And now, we are going to work on our alibi."

Langston raises an eyebrow. "I'm not fucking you, huntress."

I smile; he used my nickname.

"I'm not asking you to fuck me. Just pretend that having sex loud enough that other guests in the hallway will notice. Mess up our clothes enough so when we leave, everyone will know that we are just horny teenagers. Our entire focus was on each other, not on killing your father."

"I hate you." Langston's teeth grind together with each word.

"Make love to me, killer."

He walks over to me, stopping inches from me.

What is he doing? Is he going to kiss me? The only kiss we've had was the one when we were kids. That doesn't count. He's much more grown-up now. More experienced. This kiss could...

He puts his hands down on the bed on either side of me.

He's going to kiss me.

And then, his hands start bouncing up and down, making me and the bed shake.

I laugh.

"You aren't supposed to laugh when I fake fuck you."

I bite my lip, stifling another chuckle.

"Ooh, yea, just like that," I moan, my eyelashes fluttering as I gaze at Langston, who hasn't moved from his position.

"Louder, baby, I want the whole house to know you are mine."

"Baby? Really?" I whisper. "That's so cheesy."

He stops shaking the bed and gives me a stern look.

"Yes, Langston!" I yell a little too loudly.

He groans loudly.

Damn, it's sexier than I imagined.

And then he slams the bed hard, the headboard creaks, splitting one of the posts.

We both moan together, calling out each other's names.

Then I collapse back on the bed, exhausted like we really did fuck.

That was intense—too intense. I need to stay focused.

When I sit back up, Langston is leaning against the opposite wall, watching me.

I catch my breath and clear my throat. "Mess up your clothes a little."

He slowly starts loosening his tie.

I fuss up my hair; I let one shoulder of my dress hang down my arm and yank the front of the dress down, revealing more cleavage than before. Then I run my thumb over my lipstick, smearing it just slightly.

Langston lets out a strangled breath.

Do I affect him like he affects me?

Not possible.

It's just tension, knowing what we're about to do.

"Now, what's your plan?" Langston asks.

"To get your father to publicly kick us out to seal our alibi."

"When really…?"

"He's going to see us sneaking off to the lake behind the house."

"Where I'll kill him."

I nod slowly.

Langston walks over to me. His thumb brushes just below my lower lip.

"No one will need to see your smeared makeup to think I fucked you."

And then he takes my hand. I don't ask him what he means. I just let him lead me out of the bedroom.

"Out," his father's voice says the second we leave the bedroom.

I hide my smirk at how well my plan is working.

Langston glares at his father. "We were just leaving."

He pulls me past where his father stands in the doorway and out the front door. Our car is already waiting for us. We drive off silently, our alibi firmly in place.

Then we circle around to the back of the lake.

Langston glances at me one last time as if to thank me without actually saying the words. I completed my part of the pact, now Langston has to complete his part—killing his father.

7

LANGSTON

"Wait here, I'll lure my father down to the lake. I'll come get you when it's done," I say to Liesel as I step out of the car.

When I exit, I hear her car door slam shut.

"I told you to stay, huntress."

"I'm not going to sit in the car and wait like some damsel in distress. I might not participate in killing him, but I deserve to be involved. To watch. To see with my own eyes that he's dead. I want him gone almost as desperately as you do."

I don't want Liesel anywhere near the danger, but more than that, I don't want her to watch me kill—even a monster like my father. It will change everything between us.

Like everything hasn't changed already.

I sigh.

"Fine. But don't let him see you. Stay hidden and don't try to help. Even if things go badly, promise me you won't interfere."

She bites her bottom lip as she thinks. "I promise to only interfere if he's killing you."

"No."

"You can't expect me to just sit by and watch you die!"

I start walking away from the car into the forest of trees behind the house. She chases after me.

"Langston!"

I stop abruptly, and she slams into my back.

"I won't watch you die."

"The fact that you think there is even a chance that he'll kill me tells me all I need to know."

She huffs. "That's not fair. I think you can handle him. I'm just saying if he brings bodyguards with him, then it won't be a fair fight, and I won't just sit by and let you die."

I should be thankful for her comments, that she cares enough to not let me die. In reality, my father could bring all the men in the house with him and I would still win. Liesel doesn't know the depths of my pain. She doesn't know how Enzo, Zeke, and I have trained for a day like this. My father and the men in the house are nothing but drunk fools. They don't know how to fire a gun or win in hand-to-hand combat.

I do.

There is no way I'll lose.

"Just stay hidden," I say, and then I storm off.

Liesel stops in the brush as I walk up the hill to the house where the party is still going strong.

I stand on the edge of the patio, just past the pool, and I wait. People don't pay me any attention, but I'm not here for their attention. I'm here for one man's—my father.

Finally, I spot him at the patio bar. *Surprise, surprise.*

I make my way over, ensuring that no one notices me. I need to keep my alibi alive.

If needed, Liesel will testify that I was with her all night, making out at her house.

I come up to my father from behind.

"We need to talk," I say.

He snaps at my words, turning around as he stumbles on his feet. I'd rather do this when he's sober. I want to be able to look him in the eye and know that he understands exactly what I'm about to do to him and why when I kill him. But if I waited until he was sober, I'd be waiting forever.

"My fists will be happy to talk to you," he turns, glaring down at me.

My eyes cut to the house filled with people. "Good luck kicking my ass here without one of these people hearing. Your wife wouldn't be happy if one of her guests saw or heard you beating your son."

"No one cares about trash like you."

Just then, a couple nearby notices the tension in my father's gaze.

My father realizes he can't give me the beating he's itching to give me here.

He grabs my bicep and starts yanking me down the hill behind the house, just like I knew he would when I goaded him. He continues to hold onto me even though I'm more than capable of getting free.

We are so close to the lake now.

Just a little further.

I pull against his hold, knowing it will only make him want to yank me further.

It does. He pulls me further until we are at the edge of the water, hidden from view of the party by the rows and rows of trees. Not even the moonlight will illuminate us.

Only then do I yank my arm free of his hold. He stumbles off balance at the sudden movement.

"Drunk bastard," I mumble under my breath.

"What did you say, boy?" He regains his footing. "I told

you to leave. Your sorry ass didn't listen!" He pulls his hand back, preparing to hit me.

He won't be hitting me, not tonight. I'll never let him hit me again.

I easily duck as he takes a swing at me.

He huffs, his nostrils flare, and his eyes widen until I can see the whites of his bloodshot eyes.

I've dreamed about killing this man for so long—in so many different ways.

A gunshot to the head.

A knife to the throat.

A snap of the neck.

Right now, my mind is quickly rotating through all of my options, trying to decide which way this man deserves to die.

He tries to hit me again while I'm thinking. I take a step back and dodge his fist once again.

This time he stumbles and has to catch himself with his hand to keep from falling completely to the ground.

It's then that I realize how this monster deserves to die. He doesn't deserve anything special. It won't take much to kill him. Just one wrong step, one stumble because he's too drunk to stay upright. Then I can finish him off.

"Stop moving and take your beating like a man! You deserve it!" he shouts at me.

I step around him until I'm just in front of the water's edge.

"No son deserves to get beaten by their father."

"You're no son of mine! You're a bastard; your mother cheated on me so many times, I'm not even sure you are mine."

I wish his statement were true. I wish I wasn't his son, but we share the same eyes, the same lanky body, the same jawline—I'm his.

I stand firm as the lake sloshes at my heels, biding my time until he swings again.

On cue, he does. This time, I wait until the very last moment—until his fist almost brushes against my cheek before I move out of the way.

I watch his body fall face-first into the water. He can't catch himself; it's too late. His body hits the water hard. From the way his head bounces, he landed on a rock beneath the surface of the water.

Slowly, he tries to push himself up.

That won't be happening.

I press my foot down on top of his back, holding him down easily with my weight. He's too drunk, too weak to get me off, even though he's twice my size.

This is for everything he's done.

I watch wordlessly as he struggles beneath my foot. Every second he's one step closer to death. Each second he loses more and more oxygen. His lungs begin to fill with water. His arms stop flailing. His body stops moving.

He's dead.

I hold my foot on his back for another couple seconds—processing the moment. He's dead and I killed him.

My mind goes blank. I don't feel anything. I can't feel anything.

Then I feel her hand.

I glance down at Liesel's fingers intertwined with my own. She doesn't speak; she just guides me out of the water, away from my father's body. The whole time I was killing my father, I forgot completely about Liesel. I was so consumed by making sure my father paid for his sins.

I don't know where Liesel is leading me, and I don't care. I'd follow her anywhere.

It's not until this moment that I realize how much I needed her here with me tonight.

Finally, she stops on the edge of a hill that overlooks the lake.

We sit down.

"Thank you," I say suddenly.

She drops my hand then, as if the phrase makes her uncomfortable. Eventually she says, "You're welcome."

We sit in silence once more, both processing what happened.

"That wasn't my first kill, you know?" I say, needing her to understand what I've become—a monster.

"I know, and it doesn't matter," she whispers back.

Liesel reaches behind a nearby bush and pulls out a bottle.

"What's this?" I ask.

"Champagne I stole from the party. I thought we should celebrate."

She hands the open bottle to me. I hold it out like I'm about to make a toast.

"To one less monster walking this earth." Then I take a long swig before handing the bottle to Liesel.

"To being free and new beginnings. May that man rot in hell."

She takes a swig.

New beginnings—that's what she said.

Our eyes meet in the chill of the night. An unspoken connection we will always share rekindles between us.

I didn't realize how much I needed her here. How much I miss the girl who lived across the street from me when I had nothing. Now that I have everything money can buy, I'm still missing one thing—her.

I open my mouth to talk but then snap it shut.

Tonight isn't the night to talk to her about our future. To ask for forgiveness. To start over.

Tonight is about putting an end to this chapter of our

lives. I won't start something new with Liesel so close to my father's death. I won't let this moment define us forever.

Someday soon, though, I'll tell Liesel how I feel—and it will change our lives forever.

Instead of acknowledging how I feel, I tell another lie. "This changes nothing."

8

LIESEL

E<small>IGHTEEN</small> Y<small>EARS</small> Old

The night Langston's father died flashes in my mind. I don't know why that particular memory makes its way into my head. Maybe because I'm currently at my mother's funeral.

I thought that night was a turning point in my life. I thought things between Langston and I would change. I thought we would stop bickering and become friends again.

Instead, we continued the back and forth between liking and hating each other. Right now, all I feel toward Langston is hate.

I thought Langston's father was the biggest monster in my life. I was wrong. Mr. Pearce was barely a cockroach compared to the Godzilla I later faced.

I'm not going to think about that now. I have to focus on burying my mother. She died of an overdose on my birthday.

I release a fistful of dirt over my mother's coffin. The minster finishes speaking and starts walking back to the church, giving me some privacy.

I'm the only person who showed up to my mother's funeral.

Enzo and Zeke offered to come, but they're off training somewhere. I didn't want to bother them.

And Langston...I haven't spoken to him in a while. At first, I thought he might show up. But the short funeral came and went, and no Langston.

Stop thinking about him.

I force myself to think about my mother. About how I'll never see her again. I try to cry, really I do. But after the suffering I've been through in the last couple of years, I eventually stopped feeling pain at all. I couldn't cry even if I wanted to.

I stand another moment, trying to pay my mother her respects before I leave and never come back to this place. Too much torment has happened here. I'm about to turn when I feel his fingers brush against mine.

Chills race up my arm at his touch—that's new.

Then his fingers lock around mine.

I don't look at him. I refuse to be the first to speak.

Deep down, I'm grateful he's here, even if he is late. No one wants to bury their mother alone.

"Here," Langston says.

I glance up and see him holding a single flower—rose-like, but not quite a rose. It looks almost identical to the flower I gave him to place on his mother's grave when we buried her in this exact cemetery all those years ago.

I take the flower and place it on my mother's stone.

And then I look at Langston. I should say something—thank him, perhaps. But I don't need to use words to tell him how I'm feeling.

Langston, on the other hand, looks like he's about to spill everything inside him. He opens his mouth, "Liesel, I—"

"Hold onto that thought." I glance at my watch. "I'm

supposed to meet my lawyer at the house to go over my mother's will and decide what to do with the house."

"What house? Enzo's guest house?"

"No, she never sold our old house here, even after we moved into Enzo's guest house. I'm meeting him there."

"Oh, okay." Langston rubs the back of his neck. He's wearing a dark shirt and jeans. Langston thinks he's the devil now after everything he's done. He's right, but I wish he would become my light, my laughter, the boy I used to care for.

"We could grab a bite after, though. Meet me at the house in thirty minutes?"

He smiles tightly. "Okay."

Langston walks to his car, while I walk to mine before driving the couple blocks to the house. I get out of the car, ignoring the feelings flooding me as I walk up to the house.

I stand on the single step and knock on the door, peering over at the dried-up bush under the window. There is a car in the driveway that I expect is the lawyer's.

The door opens.

I gasp.

"Dad?" I ask the man who has my hazel eyes, my blonde hair, my complexion. He looks almost exactly like the single picture I have of him. The only difference is his hair is now peppered with gray, and he seems to have a few more wrinkles around his eyes and mouth. He shouldn't be here. He left my mom and me when I was three. He has no right to be here.

"Yes," he says.

I turn to walk away.

"Wait, please, let me explain. Talk to me; then I'll be gone and out of your life forever."

"Why should I?" I snap at him.

"Because I'll keep hunting you, stalking you until you give in and talk to me. You might as well get it over with now."

I glare, my eyes narrow in defiance, but I eventually decide to stomp inside the house. "You couldn't have chosen a different day other than my mother's funeral to talk to me?"

He shuts the door behind me and stands facing me, like he's blocking off my escape route. He doesn't know that a man like him doesn't terrify me. Nothing scares me anymore, not after I've been through hell already.

"You have five minutes, start talking," I say, folding my arms over my chest. The ratty couch I used to sleep on is still in the living room, but I refuse to sit on it.

My father doesn't either.

"I didn't come here to apologize for leaving you. Although, I am sorry to hear about your mother."

"Good, because I wouldn't forgive you." I don't acknowledge his comment about my mother.

He nods.

"I came here to tell you about your inheritance, of sorts."

I frown. "Just take the house and whatever money Mom had. I'm not going to fight you. I have my own money now."

He looks me over, head to toe, taking in my appearance, my expensive clothes. I've come a long way in a short time thanks to the help of my friends.

"I can see that. Still, it's time I told you a story."

I huff. "Really? I don't have time for a story. My friend is picking me up any minute now."

He raises an eyebrow, calling my bluff.

"I still have four minutes remaining. I can tell you the story in that amount of time."

"Go on, then."

Once upon a time, I fell in love.

She was feisty, radiant, and reckless. She had nothing. She came from nothing. And unless she found a rich husband—it would take everything she had to pull herself out of poverty.

I wasn't rich.

I had less money than her.

I had no college degree.

No job prospects.

All I had was five dollars in my pocket and the clothes on my back.

None of that mattered.

Our love was enough.

We vowed to love each other forever.

We got married.

A baby followed.

I thought our life together was so happy.

I thought we could make our marriage last.

I thought...

I thought it was enough.

Turns out, you can't live on love.

You can't eat love.

Breathe love.

Live under a roof made of love.

You need money.

We tried to make more of ourselves. I went to a community college.

It wasn't enough.

She worked three jobs.

It wasn't enough.

Our baby deserved more.

We deserved more.

So we started hunting for a way out.

Hunting.

Hunting.

Hunting...

Until finally, we found a way out.

We had more money than we could have ever imagined.

More money than the suits who used to look down on us as we cleaned their homes.

More money than the executives who those suits reported to.

More money than the queen of England.

We thought we had it all. We thought we knew what came next.

But all that came next was defending what we had stolen.

Our love wasn't enough.

Fighting our enemies wore us down until we had no energy left, no desire to fight. Until our love dissolved into ash, and our hearts were torn apart.

Sometimes fairy tales turn into nightmares.

Listen to my warning, child.

Don't search for it.

Don't seek the fairytale.

Don't seek the money like your mother and me.

Run, Liesel.

Hide.

Don't hunt.

Above everything else, don't ever tell anyone the truth—who you are or what you know.

———

"I don't understand," I say. *All this time my parents had money? They had a treasure? The only reason I grew up poor was because they weren't strong enough to keep the money?*

"It's all in here." He hands me an envelope.

I stare at it with big eyes as I begin to remove the letter from the envelope. "What is it?"

He puts his hand over mine, stopping me.

"Later. Read it later, when you're alone. Then burn it. Forget about going after the money, the treasure. Lie to anyone who asks you about it."

"I have so many questions," I say, staring at the envelope cautiously.

"I know, and I wish we had more time."

"Is this goodbye?"

"It is, my sweet daughter. It is."

He leans forward and kisses me on the cheek before I realize what's happening. I'm in shock. This man is insane. There is no way any of this is true.

"Go," he says, breaking the trance I'm under.

I take a step out of the tiny house, knowing that I won't be back inside ever again. This part of my life is over. My mother is gone, and I won't search for my father. I doubt I even read this stupid letter.

I run out, and I don't hear him following me.

I head toward my car, planning on driving away before Langston appears. I just want out of here. I can't handle a dinner with Langston right now.

But Langston is already here, and he'll stop me. I feel him before I see him.

When I look up, I see the tension on his face, a vein bulging on his forehead. He's pissed, but I don't know why.

"Is it true?" he asks me, stopping me from entering my car.

"Is what true? You're going to have to be a little more specific. My mother just died, and my father decided to show up after fifteen years of running and dropped a bomb on me."

Langston's nostrils flare.

"Is. It. True?"

"I. Don't. Know. What. You're. Talking. About." I point my finger at him as I talk.

He doesn't back down, but I don't have the patience to deal with him. I grab my car door and climb in. He catches the door right before I slam it in his face.

One tense moment.

He slams the door.

I drive away.

I'll deal with Langston later.

I look at the envelope in my hand after a few miles, deciding I should just pull over at the nearest Starbucks to read it and blow off whatever ridiculous conspiracy theory my father stumbled on in a drugged up state.

I do a double-take—the letter is torn.

Right in half.

Langston. The asshole tore the envelope when he grabbed the car door.

Dammit—I pull over and slam my hands against the steering wheel.

I take a deep breath, composing myself, and then I open the letter and read.

I read every word on my half.

The words reverberate in my core; they're true. But I only have half of the secret. Langston has the other half.

My father was worried about the treasure staying hidden. He won't have to worry, though. There is no way Langston will give up his half of the secret, and there is no way I'll give up mine to him.

The treasure is safe.

Lie, Liesel—it's the only way to stay alive.

My father meant to warn me with his words. He didn't know that lying is all I do. Lying has kept me alive, even when I wish I had died.

I laugh, staring at the letter.

There is no way any of this is true. It's all a lie, yet another lie Langston and I share. A lie we will never reveal, just like all the other lies from our past.

———

Thank you so much for reading Lies We Share: A Prologue! Langston & Liesel's story continues in Vicious Lies.

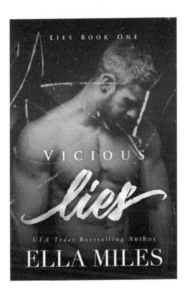

Grab Vicious Lies Here!

HAVEN'T READ ENZO AND KAI'S STORY YET? CHECK OUT THE TRUTH OR LIES SERIES BELOW:

Taken by Lies #1
Betrayed by Truths #2
Trapped by Lies #3
Stolen by Truths #4

Possessed by Lies #5
Consumed by Truths #6

HAVEN'T READ ZEKE AND SIREN'S STORY YET?
CHECK OUT THE SINFUL TRUTHS SERIES
BELOW:

Sinful Truth #1
Twisted Vow #2
Reckless Fall #3
Tangled Promise #4
Fallen Love #5
Broken Anchor #6

JOIN ELLA's NEWSLETTER & NEVER MISS A SALE
OR NEW RELEASE → ellamiles.com/freebooks

Love swag boxes & signed books?
SHOP MY STORE → store.ellamiles.com

VICIOUS LIES CHAPTER ONE

LIESEL

I WILL KILL YOU.

I read the words on the piece of paper in my hand. *Who puts death threats in the mail anymore?* It seems archaic and old-timey. There are so many better ways to send a threat: a phone call, a text message, an email.

An in-person act of violence really sends a message too, if you really have the balls.

Why write a letter?

Because he's a coward.

I consider tossing the letter in the trash and not taking the issue any further, forgetting that it even happened. But I didn't survive this long by tossing away idle threats.

I will kill you.

This isn't the first time someone has made a threat like this against me.

I will kill everyone you love.

Again, not new. I just thought I was passed this part of my life. I thought I was done living in this dangerous, vicious world. One where there are no winners—at least, I never win. I just survive.

I thought, just like letter writing, this part of my life was buried in the past.

I tap my painted red nails against my desk as I read the letter over two more times. Nothing hints at who the author is. There is no name scrolled across the bottom. Like I thought—*wuss*.

But that doesn't mean there aren't hints of who my enemy is. The way the letter is scribed tells me it's a man who wrote it. It was scribbled quickly with a pen almost out of ink on a piece of computer paper. This note was written last minute; it wasn't thought through.

And it didn't arrive in an envelope in the mail. It was stuffed loosely into the mailbox. I wouldn't be surprised if I found fingerprints.

Whoever sent this is an amateur, or at least, wants me to think he's an amateur.

I'm not an amateur. As much as I never thought I would know how to hold a gun, fire a weapon, hunt down men, rescue myself, I've never had a choice in the matter. My entire life I've lived in a cruel underworld of men who controlled everything. Men who had no right to own anything. Men who ruled with guns and darkness in their hearts, taking no prisoners. Taking what they wanted without concern of whom they hurt.

I used to be a princess in a world filled with dangerous men. I used to have friends who would protect me above everything else.

But things started slowly changing when my best friend, Enzo Black, fell in love. And then Zeke, my other protector, fell in love next. It's only a matter of time until Langston, the playboy of the group, falls in love.

I could call any one of them to take care of the man who sent this threat. Enzo, Zeke, or Langston all have the power and abilities to handle this man without lifting a finger.

That's what they do—kill dangerous men. They protect their family, which used to include me.

Until they failed me.

Until they fell in love.

Until I decided I didn't want to be a damsel in distress, waiting for a man to come and rescue me.

I saved myself.

I picked up every broken, shattered piece and put myself back together, painstakingly, piece by piece.

I'm whole now—even if the pieces don't fit together the same as they did before.

I'm a survivor—that's the term used to describe me. It's a term I hate, because I didn't just survive, I thrived. I fought back; I rescued myself. I'm a fucking knight in red high heels.

So while I could call my friends to save me and take care of this, I'm not going to. I haven't asked any one of them for help in years, and I'm not going to start now.

I lift my glass of scotch from my desk and swirl it around until the single ball of ice shifts in the glass, making a delicious rattling sound before I take a sip. I'm a woman in a man's world, but that doesn't mean I let the men rule me anymore. I won't give any man power over me—never again.

So that leaves me two choices. I can toss this letter in the trash and ignore it completely. There is a large chance whoever sent it will never grow enough balls to actually act on his threat. Or I go back into the world I never thought I would enter again.

A world of danger.

Cruelty.

Vows.

And lies.

A world that once consumed me. A world that turned me into the cold, heartless woman I've become. A world that took everything from me, yet gave me my power.

I thought I was done.

I thought this chapter of my life was over, buried.

I could leave it alone. For years, I've done everything I can to stay out of this life. To stay away from the evil that lurks in the night. Not because I'm afraid of the darkness hurting me. Not because I'm afraid that the man making the threat will actually succeed. Even if he did succeed, I'm not afraid of death.

No, I've stayed away from the darkness because I haven't wanted to become the villain I'm capable of being. Once the darkness surrounds me, I'll no longer be the princess. I'll become the evil queen. Once I let it in, there is no way to get it out. That's why I've put up walls around my heart, to keep the vile out, the wickedness I can become.

But why?

Why can't I turn into the evil queen?

My friends and family are gone. The only man in my life is more than capable of taking care of himself.

I shouldn't go back to this life.

I should crumple the letter up and toss it into the fireplace to burn.

I should forget the threat until it comes true.

But I feel the walls lowering around my heart. All the men in my life are able to stay safe and protect those they love, because they don't fight the worst parts of themselves.

Enzo is a controlling bastard, who rules his world by loving Kai.

Zeke protects those he loves no matter the cost it inflicts on himself.

And Langston hurts others to protect himself.

All three men have done more than survived; they've become kings. They've languished and destroyed their enemies. They've gained enough power that no man dares to make threats like this.

It's time I try their tactics.

I toss the rest of the scotch back into my throat before slamming the glass down on my desk with a sinful grin across my red-painted lips.

The evil that I locked in my heart is free. I'm going to use every bit of its power to take care of this threat myself, so no man or woman will ever threaten me again.

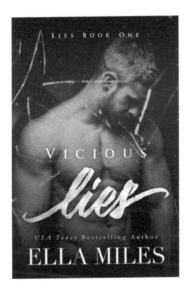

Grab Vicious Lies Here!

ALSO BY ELLA MILES

LIES SERIES:

Lies We Share: A Prologue

Vicious Lies

Desperate Lies

Fated Lies

Cruel Lies

Dangerous Lies

Endless Lies

SINFUL TRUTHS:

Sinful Truth #1

Twisted Vow #2

Reckless Fall #3

Tangled Promise #4

Fallen Love #5

Broken Anchor #6

TRUTH OR LIES:

Taken by Lies #1

Betrayed by Truths #2

Trapped by Lies #3

Stolen by Truths #4

Possessed by Lies #5

Consumed by Truths #6

DIRTY SERIES:

Dirty Obsession

Dirty Addiction

Dirty Revenge

Dirty: The Complete Series

ALIGNED SERIES:

Aligned: Volume 1 (Free Series Starter)

Aligned: Volume 2

Aligned: Volume 3

Aligned: Volume 4

Aligned: The Complete Series Boxset

UNFORGIVABLE SERIES:

Heart of a Thief

Heart of a Liar

Heart of a Prick

Unforgivable: The Complete Series Boxset

ABOUT THE AUTHOR

Ella Miles writes steamy romance, including everything from dark suspense romance that will leave you on the edge of your seat to contemporary romance that will leave you laughing out loud or crying. Most importantly, she wants you to feel everything her characters feel as you read.

Ella is currently living her own happily ever after near the Rocky Mountains with her high school sweetheart husband. Her heart is also taken by her goofy five year old black lab who is scared of everything, including her own shadow.

Ella is a USA Today Bestselling Author & Top 50 Bestselling Author.

Stalk Ella at:
www.ellamiles.com
ella@ellamiles.com

Lightning Source UK Ltd.
Milton Keynes UK
UKHW010042170223
417092UK00003B/201

9 781951 114732